This book is dedicated to

ALL the Children of the World

both young and old.

May you all be blessed with knowing yourself as a gift of God.

Thanks God, I Love You, and Goodnight

Korinn S. Hawkins

Thank you God for today,
A blessing to me in everyway.

For Everything in my life you give,

I am grateful for my chance to live.

Thank you God for
family and friends,

For all the fun and
sometimes a challenge.

Thank you God for new
experiences and
opportunities to grow,
To listen, and to learn, and
discover what is to know.

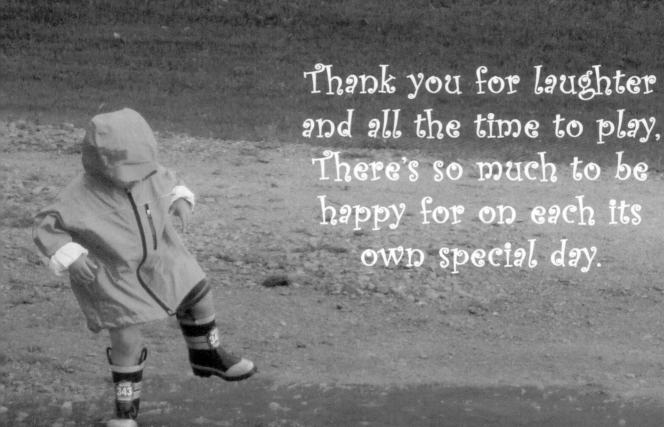

Thank you for laughter
and all the time to play,
There's so much to be
happy for on each its
own special day.

Thank you for your guidance,
for your beauty, and your love,

Helping me to see that everything
has purpose from above.

Even when it's hard to understand why,
I know a reason does exist,

For every message and
lesson learned
is sealed by
Heaven's
kiss.

How else would I know my strength if I never had to fall, How else would I know you were there if I never had to call.

So thank you God for being with me every moment of each day,

Thank you for
the Earth, for the
water, air,
and light,

All these things we
need that bless us
to live our life.

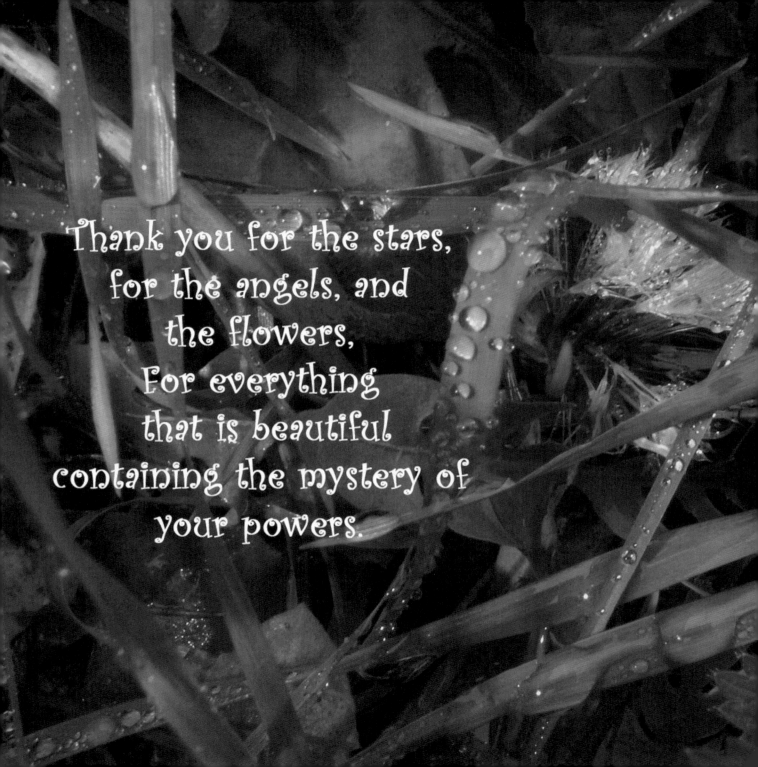

Thank you for the stars,
for the angels, and
the flowers,
For everything
that is beautiful
containing the mystery of
your powers.

Thank you for being present
and for giving me
free choice,

It is my body that takes action from my heart that shares your voice.

Thank you for allowing me
this peace I feel inside,
Inspired by the presence
of you here by my side.

I know that I am blessed
as I close this book
and turn off the light,

You are here all around me
so Thanks God,
I Love You,
and Goodnight.

Now look around you
and tell me
where is it that
you see
God
right now?...

5205553R0

Made in the USA
Charleston, SC
13 May 2010